A Note to Parents

DK CLASSIC READERS is a compelling program for beginning readers, designed in conjunction with leading literacy experts, including Dr. Linda Gambrell, Director of the School of Education at Clemson University. Dr. Gambrell has served on the Board of Directors of the International Reading Association and as President of the National Reading Conference.

Beautiful illustrations and superb full-color photographs combine with engaging, easy-to-read stories to offer a fresh approach to each subject in the series. Each DK CLASSIC READER is guaranteed to capture a child's interest while developing his or her reading skills, general knowledge, and love of reading.

The four levels of DK CLASSIC READERS are aimed at different reading abilities, enabling you to choose the books that are exactly right for your child:

Level 1: Beginning to read
Level 2: Beginning to read alone
Level 3: Reading alone
Level 4: Proficient readers

The "normal" age at which a child begins to read can be anywhere from three to eight years old, so these levels are intended only as a general guideline.

No matter which level you select, you can be sure that you are helping your child learn to read, then read to learn!

LONDON, NEW YORK, MUNICH,
MELBOURNE, and DELHI

Created by Leapfrog Press Ltd

Project Editor Naia Bray-Moffatt
Art Editor Miranda Kennedy

For Dorling Kindersley
Senior Editor Marie Greenwood
Managing Art Editor Jacquie Gulliver
Managing Editor Joanna Devereux
Production Chris Augherinos
Picture Researcher Liz Moore
Cover design Margherita Gianni

Reading Consultant
Linda B. Gambrell, Ph.D.

First American Edition, 2000
04 05 06 10 9 8 7 6 5 4 3 2
Published in the United States by DK Publishing, Inc.
375 Hudson Street, New York, New York 10014

Dorling Kindersley Classic Readers™ is a trademark
of Dorling Kindersley Limited

Published in Great Britain by Dorling Kindersley Limited

A catalog record is available from the Library of Congress.

ISBN 0-7894-5390-8

Color reproduction by Colourscan, Singapore
Printed and bound in Belgium by Proost

The publisher would like to thank the following for their kind
permission to reproduce their photographs:
Key b = below.
AKG London: 27, 33b; Bridgeman Art Library: 45; Bruce
Coleman Collection: 6; Science & Society Picture Library: 37.
All other images © Dorling Kindersley.
For further information see: www.dkimages.com

Discover more at

www.dk.com

Contents

CLASSIC READERS

 READING 3 ALONE

HEIDI

A TIMELESS STORY OF CHILDHOOD

By Johanna Spyri

Adapted by Lucy Coats   Illustrated by Pamela Venus

DK Publishing, Inc.

Up the mountain

One June morning, Heidi trudged up the mountain behind her Aunt Detie. Heidi's parents were dead and Detie couldn't look after her anymore.

Detie was taking
Heidi to live with
her grandfather.

They climbed
high up the
mountain to a
wooden hut in
some fir trees,
where an old man
was sitting on a
rough bench.

Heidi ran up to
him. "Hello, Grandfather!" she said.
The old man stared at her.

"Here is the child, Uncle," said Detie.
"She must stay with you now."

"Ho!" said Grandfather, frowning.
"She must, must she? Well leave her
here and go away then!"

Wooden home

Heidi went to live in the mountains of Switzerland, called the Alps. Mountain huts, like Grandfather's, were made of strong wood to keep out the wind and the cold.

Heidi began to explore her new home. She peeped into the goat stall, ran around the three fir trees and then went indoors with Grandfather.

"Where shall I sleep?" she asked.

"Wherever you like, child," replied Grandfather.

Heidi wanted to sleep in the loft. Soon she and Grandfather had made a cozy bed out of soft hay.

"It's just perfect!" Heidi exclaimed.

"Time to eat now," said Grandfather. He put some toasted bread and cheese in front of her and Heidi ate hungrily. She couldn't believe how good everything tasted.

As dusk fell, a boy called Peter appeared with Grandfather's goats. Heidi said goodnight to her new friends and skipped happily up to bed.

Mountain goats

Goats feed on grass and shrubs. In summer, goatherds lead their herds up the mountains to feed on fresh pastures.

Early the next morning, Heidi and Peter took the goats to the grassy pasture. Heidi ran around the meadow picking flowers. Peter taught her the names of all the goats. Her favorite was a little white goat called Snowflake.

On the way home, Heidi cried out in amazement. The mountains seemed to be on fire!

But Grandfather told her it was only the sun saying goodnight.

Grandfather told Heidi
more stories of the
mountains while
she ate her
supper.

Winter soon came
and one day it snowed heavily.
Grandfather wrapped Heidi up warmly
and they sledded down the side of the
mountain to visit Peter's Granny.

"Here I am, Granny!" called Heidi.
The old lady held out her hands.

"Come to me, my child, for I can't
see you."

"Let me open the shutters, Granny. Then you will see me." The old woman shook her head sadly and told Heidi that she was blind. Heidi was sorry for her and promised to come and see her every day.

So all winter long Heidi kept Granny company, while Grandfather repaired her rickety old hut.

Aunt Detie visits

In the early spring,
Aunt Detie visited Heidi
and Grandfather again.
She said that she was taking
Heidi to Frankfurt to be a
companion to a little girl
who was in a wheelchair.
The girl had no mother
and her father was often
away, so she
was lonely.

Train journey

Trains were the quickest kind of transportation in those days. But it still took Heidi about two days to travel across Europe from the Swiss Alps to her new home in Frankfurt.

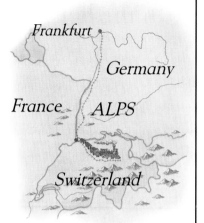

Frankfurt

Germany

France   ALPS

Switzerland

Grandfather was furious with Detie.

"Heidi's healthy and happy where she is," he said.

"I won't come! I won't!" yelled poor Heidi. "I want to stay here with Grandfather." But it was no use.

A determined Aunt Detie packed Heidi's clothes and dragged the crying girl down the mountain and aboard the train. Heidi did not even have time to say goodbye to anyone.

In the house in Frankfurt, Clara Sesemann sat with Miss Rottenmeier, the housekeeper, waiting for her new friend. Soon there was a knock at the door and Heidi and Aunt Detie arrived. Miss Rottenmeier was rather unhappy about Heidi's shabby clothes.

"She really will not do at all!" she said.

Heidi and Clara soon made friends, but Heidi was still homesick. Everything here was strange, even suppertime.

This was not like Grandfather's hut at all. Miss Rottenmeier gave her a long lecture on how to behave, but Heidi was so tired that she fell asleep in the middle of it.

Lesson-time the next morning was worse. Heidi heard a rustling like the wind through the fir trees at home. She ran to the window, knocking over an inkwell in her hurry to see the trees, but it was only some carriages passing. Clara laughed, but Miss Rottenmeier was furious with Heidi.

While Clara rested after lunch, Heidi went out to explore. She soon found a church with a high tower and begged the caretaker to let her climb to the top. But all she could see were chimneys and roofs instead of her beloved mountains.

Seeing how sad Heidi looked, the caretaker gave her some kittens.

"Take two now and I'll deliver the rest," he said. Heidi was delighted and skipped home with them in her pocket.

The next morning a basket appeared for Heidi at lesson-time. Clara wanted to know what was inside, and she didn't have to wait long. The lid was not properly fastened, and suddenly there were kittens everywhere.

"Oh look! How pretty," exclaimed Clara, as one climbed onto her knee. But some of them tried to claw their way up Miss Rottenmeier's skirt.

She screamed and danced around the floor in terror.

"Oh! Oh! Oh! Get rid of these horrible creatures!" She turned to Heidi. "You dreadful child! You shall be shut up in the cellar with the rats as your punishment!"

But Clara said, "Oh, please wait until Papa comes home. I promise to tell him everything. Let him decide what should happen to Heidi."

Reluctantly, Miss Rottenmeier agreed.

For a few days afterward, nothing else went wrong. But this did not stop Heidi from feeling homesick. She missed Grandfather and Granny and the sun saying goodnight to the mountains. She decided to run away. She packed up all her belongings and was about to set off when she met Miss Rottenmeier.

"Where do you think you're going?" demanded Miss Rottenmeier.

"Home," said Heidi bravely.

"You ungrateful child!" scolded Miss Rottenmeier, as she snatched her bundle away. "Look at these things! They're a disgrace and I shall throw them in the trash can."

Heidi cried and cried at the loss of her precious belongings, and even Clara and the kittens could not comfort her.

Mr. Sesemann

A few days later, Clara's father arrived home from his travels abroad.

Miss Rottenmeier soon had a word with him.

"Heidi's behavior is terrible, and she brings dreadful animals into the house. I think she is crazy!"

"She seems normal enough to me," said Mr. Sesemann. "But I shall ask Clara what she thinks."

Clara told him about the inkwell and the kittens. Her father laughed.

"So you don't want Heidi to go home then?"

"Oh no, Papa!"

Mr. Sesemann went back to see Miss Rottenmeier.

"Heidi will stay," he said firmly. "Clara loves having her here. And I shall ask my mother to look after Heidi when she arrives next week."

The next week, Grandmamma Sesemann arrived. She sat down with Heidi and put her arm around her.

"What have you learned in your lessons, my dear?" she asked.

"Nothing," sighed Heidi. "Reading is too difficult!"

Grandmamma smiled. "If you work hard, I will give you this book!"

The book had beautiful pictures of meadows and mountains that reminded Heidi of home. Her eyes shined. "I wish I could read now!" she exclaimed.

One morning, about a week later, Grandmamma peeped into the study. There was Heidi reading to Clara!

"I can do it! I can read!" she cried.

That evening, Heidi found the beautiful book by her place at supper.

"It is yours for always," said Grandmamma.

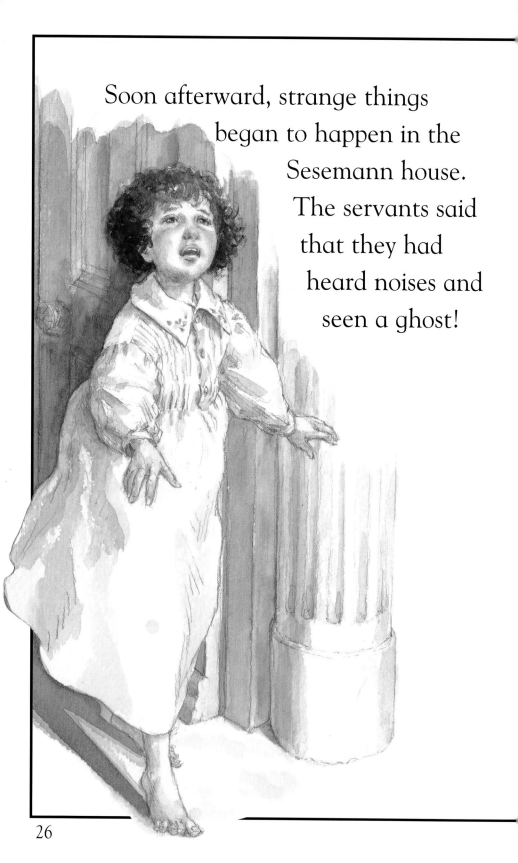

Soon afterward, strange things
began to happen in the
Sesemann house.
The servants said
that they had
heard noises and
seen a ghost!

Mr. Sesemann decided to investigate with his friend, Dr. Classen. Late one night they saw a little white figure in the moonlight.

"Who's there?" they shouted.

The figure turned around. It was Heidi.

"Have you been dreaming?" asked Dr. Classen.

"Oh yes," said Heidi. "I dreamed I was with Grandfather. But then I woke up and I'm still here!" She began to cry.

Dr. Classen talked to Mr. Sesemann.

"Heidi is terribly homesick. You must send her back right away!"

Sleepwalking
People may walk while they are sleeping. They can't remember sleepwalking when they wake up.

Home again

Heidi couldn't believe that she was going home at last. Clara promised Heidi that she would visit and they kissed goodbye.

The long train journey passed in a flash and soon Heidi was running into Peter's hut and hugging Granny.

Grandfather was sitting on the bench outside his hut, just as he had been when Heidi first saw him. Heidi ran to him crying, "Grandfather!" and threw her arms around him. Both their eyes were wet with tears.

"So you've come back then," he said. "Did they send you away?"

"Oh no," said Heidi. She tried to tell Grandfather what had happened, then gave him a letter from Mr. Sesemann which explained everything.

There was a shrill whistle from the mountainside. It was Peter and the goats. He stared at Heidi, amazed.

"I'm so glad you're home," he said.

Grandfather woke Heidi at sunrise the next day.

"Get up, Heidi! We are going to church." At the end of the service Grandfather spoke to the pastor.

"I have decided that Heidi will go to school this winter and we will move down to my old house in the village."

The pastor smiled and welcomed them.

One morning Dr. Classen arrived. He explained that Clara had been very ill and couldn't come to visit until the summer. He brought presents and food from her and soon Grandfather had prepared a wonderful picnic.

Dr. Classen ate hungrily. "Clara will certainly get well when she comes here!" he exclaimed.

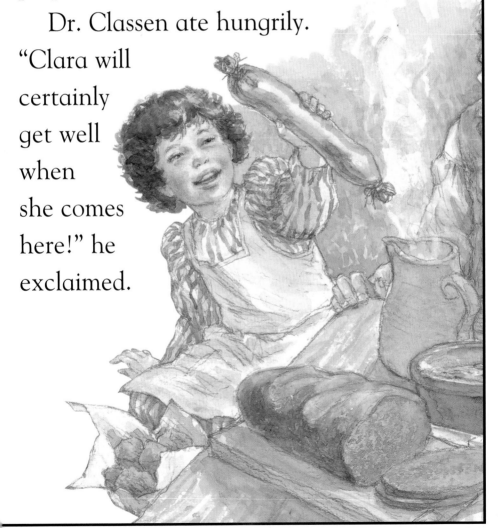

That winter, as promised,
Grandfather and Heidi moved down to
an old house in the village.

Every morning Heidi went to school
and worked hard. But Peter always
played hooky. He didn't like
lessons. Grandfather got
very angry with him.

Granny was ill
when Heidi next
went to visit.

"Poor
Granny,"
she said.

"I wish that I could read to you every day."

Then Heidi had a brilliant idea. She would teach Peter to read to Granny. Peter reluctantly agreed. Heidi began by teaching him his alphabet from a book Clara had given her. Then one day Peter astonished Granny by reading her a whole hymn. He was very proud.

Alphabet book
Heidi helped Peter learn his letters with a German alphabet book like this. Knowing his ABCs helped Peter learn to read.

Clara comes to stay

One spring morning, when Heidi and Grandfather had moved back to the hut, Peter brought them a letter from Frankfurt. Heidi opened it.

"Clara is coming!" Heidi cried excitedly. "Hooray!"

But Peter was not so pleased. He was frightened that Heidi would go away and leave him again.

Weeks later, Heidi and Grandfather saw a strange procession of people climbing the mountainside. "They've come!" she cried and ran to meet them.

Grandfather lifted Clara into her wheelchair.

Heidi pushed her all around the hut.

"How lovely it is," cried Clara, as Grandfather carried her up to show her Heidi's hayloft. "Can I sleep here, too?"

Grandmamma arranged to stay in the nearby village and agreed to come and visit soon. The two girls were overjoyed.

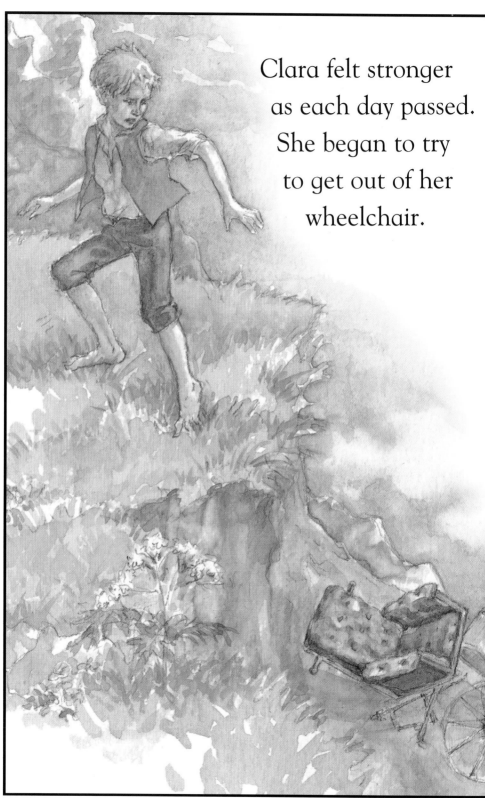

Clara felt stronger
as each day passed.
She began to try
to get out of her
wheelchair.

Wheelchair

Many people with disabilities could not afford wheelchairs. Clara was lucky that she could. She had a wheelchair that was made specially for her.

Soon she begged to go to the pasture with the goats. But Peter was jealous.

One morning, Peter saw Clara's empty wheelchair outside the hut. In a rage, he hurled it down the steep slope. Now Clara would have to go home, he thought to himself. Then he ran away without even waiting for the goats.

When Grandfather came around the corner carrying Clara he looked everywhere for the wheelchair. But it was nowhere to be found.

When they found the smashed wheelchair, Clara cried, because now she wouldn't be able to go to the pasture. Grandfather hated to see her so upset and decided to carry Clara all the way to the pasture himself.

When they arrived, Peter was already there, and Grandfather asked if he had seen Clara's chair. "No," said Peter, but Grandfather looked at him thoughtfully.

Clara and Heidi spent a happy morning playing with the goats. After lunch, Heidi wanted to show Clara the lovely flowers in the meadow higher up. She asked Peter to help her lift Clara, and he felt so guilty that he agreed.

With Heidi and Peter's help, Clara put one foot in front of the other.

"Look!" she exclaimed. "I can walk!"

Grandfather was delighted.

Clara practiced her walking every day until Grandmamma's next visit. Grandmamma stared in amazement as Clara walked slowly toward her.

"How can I ever thank you? It's a miracle!" she gasped to Grandfather.

"Just God's sun and good mountain air!" Grandfather smiled back.

One afternoon, as Peter was going to the village, he met a stranger who asked him the way to Heidi's hut.

"A policeman, coming to arrest me for smashing the chair," thought Peter, as he ran away, terrified.

"What an odd, shy boy," said Mr. Sesemann to himself as he continued on his way up the mountain.

Clara's father laughed to himself as he got closer to Grandfather's hut. His business trip had finished early and he was looking forward to surprising Clara. "They'll have such a shock when they see me!" he chuckled. But it was

Mr. Sesemann who had the shock instead.

As he came nearer the hut he stood and stared, and his eyes filled with tears.

"Don't you know me, Papa?" cried Clara, walking straight toward him.

"Is it possible?" he whispered, as he took her in his arms. Then Grandmamma joined them.

"You must meet Heidi's grandfather."

While Mr. Sesemann thanked Grandfather from the bottom of his heart for helping Clara to walk, Grandmamma saw Peter sneaking by.

"Young man," she called. "Why are you looking so guilty?" Peter turned red, blushing with shame as he confessed about Clara's wheelchair.

"What you did was very wrong," said Grandmamma. "But since you are sorry for what you did, you are forgiven."

Grandmamma understood how jealous Peter had been of Clara's friendship with Heidi. Then she asked him what he would like as a present to remember them by. For the first time in his life, Peter could have anything he wanted. He thought and thought, then he asked for a penny. Grandmamma laughed and promised him a penny a week for life. Peter couldn't believe his luck and skipped away, overjoyed!

Later, Mr. Sesemann asked Grandfather how he could reward him for all he had done for his daughter.

"It is reward enough to see Clara so well," said Grandfather. "But if you promise me that you will take care of Heidi when I die, that would make me very happy," said Grandfather, and the two men shook hands on it.

All too soon the time came for Clara, Mr. Sesemann, and Grandmamma to say goodbye, but Clara promised to visit them next summer.

One penny

Peter could buy as much with a penny as you can buy with $15 now. This is an English penny from the time Heidi's story was written.

That was not the end of the story. Shortly afterward, Dr. Classen retired and bought Grandfather's old ramshackle house in the village. He had it rebuilt so that Heidi and Grandfather could still live in one half during winter. Grandfather became the doctor's best friend and taught him all the ways of the mountains.

"Heidi seems like my own daughter," he said to Grandfather one day. "May I help you take care of her?"

Grandfather shook his hand. "That would be wonderful," he smiled.

So Heidi spent another happy winter down in the village.

There she was
surrounded by
people who
loved and
cared for her.

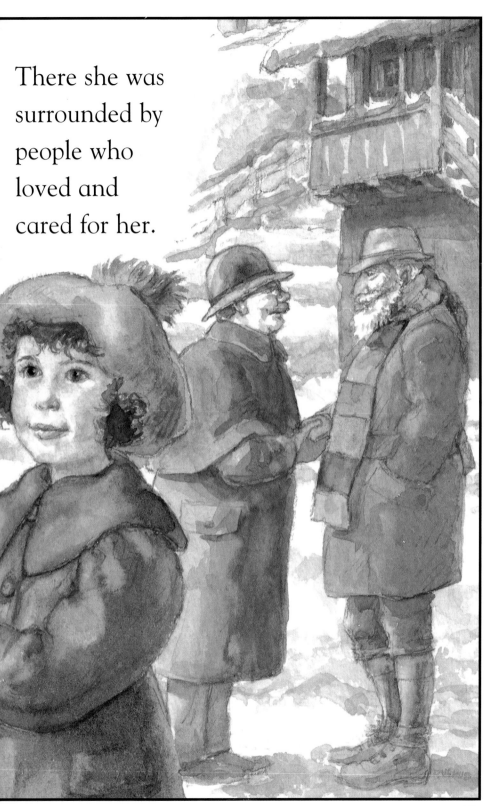

Glossary

Alps
A range of high mountains in Europe. The Alps stretch across many countries, including Switzerland, France, Germany, Italy, Austria, and what used to be Yugoslavia.

Carriage
A vehicle with wheels used for carrying people, usually drawn by horses. Carriages have now been replaced by cars.

Determined
A determined person has set his or her mind on something and will not change it.

Goatherd
A person who raises many goats for wool and for milk, which may be made into delicious cheese.

Guilty
A guilty person has done something wrong or feels that he or she has behaved badly.

Hay
Grass or another such plant that has been cut and dried for feeding animals. Hay may be stored in a hayloft.

Hooky
Children who play hooky do not go to school when they should.

Housekeeper
A person hired to manage someone else's home. A housekeeper often lives in the home they manage.

Hymn
A song praising God. Hymns are often sung during religious ceremonies such as church services.

Inkwell
A pot that holds ink. Ink pens are dipped in an inkwell and filled with ink before writing.

Pastor
A member of the clergy who is in charge of a church. A pastor may also be called a priest or a minister.

Pasture
The grassy land where sheep and cattle can graze.

Sleepwalking
When a person gets up and walks or even talks while they are sleeping.